The Wanderer
A Political Fable

R. Michael Hoy

National Library of Canada Cataloguing in Publication Data

Hoy, R. Michael
The wanderer : a political fable / R. Michael Hoy.
ISBN 1-55395-777-6
I. Title.
PS3608.O899W35 2003 813'.6
C2003-900719-7

TRAFFORD

This book was published *on-demand* in cooperation with Trafford Publishing.
On-demand publishing is a unique process and service of making a book available for retail sale to the public taking advantage of on-demand manufacturing and Internet marketing. **On-demand publishing** includes promotions, retail sales, manufacturing, order fulfilment, accounting and collecting royalties on behalf of the author.

Suite 6E, 2333 Government St., Victoria, B.C. V8T 4P4, CANADA
Phone 250-383-6864 Toll-free 1-888-232-4444 (Canada & US)
Fax 250-383-6804 E-mail sales@trafford.com
Web site www.trafford.com TRAFFORD PUBLISHING IS A DIVISION OF TRAFFORD HOLDINGS LTD.
Trafford Catalogue #03-0140 www.trafford.com/robots/03-0140.html

10 9 8 7 6 5 4 3 2 1

This book is dedicated to my wife Carol whose support during its development was invaluable.

Acknowledgements

- The interpretive skills and outstanding illustrations by Heather Price were an integral part of this fable.
- My everlasting gratitude to Eileen Sullivan whose editorial skills were priceless in bringing this fable to fruition.

Chapter I

ooking back, not only was his arrival unheralded, but no one seemed to know when he arrived. Nevertheless, one day he appeared in the marketplace of the kingdom, wandering the streets and querying the local citizens. The more people to whom he spoke, the more he felt a restlessness in their responses to his questions. The kingdom and its citizens appeared to be prosperous, but there was an ominous uneasiness in their presence. With this seeming contradiction, he decided to delve into the problem.

He decided first to see who ruled this kingdom. This, he felt, would be the appropriate place to begin his search. This in mind, he asked one of the citizens where he might find the rulers. This was accomplished fairly easily when the citizen pointed to an enormous white palace surrounded by vast grounds and enclosed by an endless high wall. The palace guard attended the entrance, but interestingly, access to the palace was allowed on a limited basis to permit the citizens to observe how the laws of the land were enacted.

As the wanderer approached the gated palace, he was directed across the spacious grounds to a spectacular hall. As he entered the hall, its interior was grandly designed, and the ornate interior matched the elegance of the multitude of well-dressed legislators in the hall. The grand hall was divided into four sections. The first was a gallery at the rear of the hall, apparently designed for the citizen observers. The second and third areas were the two sides of the hall, with an equal number of legislators on either side. The fourth section was at the far end, and consisted of three levels of finely crafted wooden benches, all of which were elevated above the other sections of the grand hall. The legislators occupying these benches seemed to be the leaders, and directed the ongoing legislative procedures.

After listening and observing this legislative gathering for several hours, certain routines became apparent to him. First, one side of the hall seemed to believe one way, and the other side seemed to have a contrary opinion. The leaders occupying the elevated levels of benches at the far end of the hall seemed to one degree or another to approve and disapprove both sides. The ongoing debating at times became heated, and at other times seemed at best laborious.

At this particular gathering, the debating seemed to involve two areas of concern. First was the question of how to subsidize the elderly who were no longer gainfully employed in the workplace. Second was how their medical costs were to be paid. Their costs increased as they got older, and the elderly could not pay for these services since they were no longer earning wages. The debate continued on inconclusively for several hours longer until the session was formally ended for that day.

Upon leaving the hall, he queried one of the citizens who was in the gallery as to why the problems were so hard to resolve and the debating seemed endless. He believed that the elderly, after leading long and productive lives, should be cared for by the wage-earning citizens if they could not support themselves. He further remarked that it seemed that the legislators should understand that they, too, would grow old and might need this assistance, so it would benefit them to solve the problem more expeditiously. The citizen turned to him puzzlingly and asked if he wasn't aware that the legislators had their own retirement and medical programs separate from the citizens. Through further questioning, he became aware that not only were the programs for the legislators better funded; in addition, their retirement program was at a much higher remuneration. He now understood why the debating was so laborious and didn't seem to get resolved. Since the legislators already had their benefits secured, it was easier to debate inconclusively without a time frame to solve the problem. If the legislators' benefits were equally involved and funded with the citizens' benefits, he surmised, the problem would have been resolved in a much more forthright manner. He was now beginning to perceive the depth of the citizenry's dilemma.

Chapter II

s he exited the palace grounds with these new thoughts in his mind, he was so fascinated by the legislative process that he returned for many sessions so that he might familiarize himself with how this process functioned.

Eventually, he came to view the legislative process as theatre of sorts. A bill would come before the legislature, and each side took a position for or against the bill. Openly each side took a hard position for their performance before the gallery of citizens; however, behind the scenes, both would negotiate some sort of middle ground. Implicit in the compromising procedure were some givens. First, one side would have to win the debate, and one side would have to lose, even if the outcome didn't suit either side. The legislator who won would say that he didn't get all of his legislation through, but if he didn't compromise part of it, he would have lost. This "partial win" approach would keep the legislator on the other side of the hall satisfied, and at the same time keep the citizens who supported him satisfied. Second, whatever legislation eventually passed would increase the size of the budget to support this new legislation, therefore increasing the size of government. Now therein was one of the basic problems. One legislative body called for more governmental programs, and the other called for smaller government. So regardless of their arguments about more services for the citizens or smaller government, because of the process, government kept growing and the new programs were only partially implemented due to the compromising nature of the process.

An important by-product of this process was, of course, higher taxes to implement these programs. As the programs became larger and more complex, the legislators required more control to maintain the growth and as a result their roles became more significant and their personal remuneration increased.

What became clear to the wanderer was that the system worked as follows. Through the "legislative process" programs grew, and at each stage of growth, three elements emerged: (1) increased taxes to the citizenry to support the changes, (2) a portion of the increased taxes would go to the legislators, increasing their salaries and staff to manage the new programs and thus increasing their positions of control, and (3) the only imperative was that government was always increasing in size, the only significant difference between the legislative bodies was that one might call for a smaller increase.

Now that he felt he had a deepe r understanding of how the government was managed, his interest turned to the citizenry and how they responded to the ever-growing governmental control with its accompanying increasing taxes.

He had been staying at a lodge conveniently located near the palace....he could intermingle with the local citizens to better understand how they dealt with their daily village existence.

Chapter III

e had been staying at a lodge conveniently located near the palace, which simplified his daily sojourn when he attended legislative meetings. Now that his time was free from these daily visits to the palace, he could intermingle with the local citizens to better understand how they dealt with their daily village existence.

How to initiate his investigation into the lifestyle of the local citizenry turned out to be more difficult than he had originally envisioned, for the citizens seemed to be so busy and preoccupied, it was difficult to dialogue with them. They seemed to be either coming from or going to some destinati on, and if this wasn't the case, they appeared so intense or preoccupied with their thoughts, that he did not dare approach them fearing that he might be rebuffed.

One morning while the wanderer was having his morning repast, he noticed an elderly citizen, sitting alone at a nearby table, who did not seem to be as preoccupied as were most of the other citizens. He decided to approach the citizen, and through him acquaint himself with the nature of life in the village.

As they began their dialogue, the citizen seemed to dwell on the past, and how it used to be so simple and uncluttered in terms of surviving the daily routine. In the past, he noted, the father went out to work, while the mother stayed at home caring for the children and maintaining the household. One day, overnight it seemed to him, two salaries were needed to support their lifestyle. He didn't know how or exactly when, but now both parents had to be out in the workplace and this caused major disruptions. As he spoke to the citizen, the wanderer reflected upon the legislative process he had witnessed in the palace and understood clearly why this basic change had occurred. While the citizenry were working, the legislative body, through its "invisible hand," had created a new equation. Due to its rapid growth and endless appetite for power and control, the government was increasing its size at such a rate that corresponding taxes to the citizens were increasing much faster than the citizens' ability to adjust to the growth. Therefore the citizens needed more money to sustain the integrity of the family. So even though the citizens were acquiring more "things" in their households, the proportion allotted to taxes and other fees was increasing at a much more rapid rate because of the insatiable appetite of the government, which required more and more taxes. What was becoming clear was that the astronomical growth of government was outstripping the ability of a family to support itself by traditional methods. People were becoming more and more busy because of economic pressures and having less and less time to watch and critique this growth of the leviathan. The government was spending all of its time planning its growth and control of the citizenry, while the citizens had to spend most of their time working to keep pace with these governmental taxes levied upon them. Was it not surprising that the citizens did not have the time or inclination to spend time talking to the wanderer?

Chapter IV

y this time, the wanderer and the elderly citizen had become comfortable with each other, and the elderly citizen suggested that he meet his son and his family on a Sunday morning, the one day when time was available for a family gathering.

The family home was down the road from the inn, within walking distance from where they had been sharing their discussions. The cottage was attractive in appearance and the grounds were well manicured, indicating that the family apparently enjoyed their abode. Upon meeting the family, they seemed less stressed, at least on the surface, than the other citizens he had encountered. Maybe this was due to the fact that the elderly citizen had discussed their morning get-togethers with the family, thereby facilitating the meeting.

The couple's son and daughter were in their adolescent years, and after brief introductions, they left to meet with their friends to do those busy things which young people are prone to do. The children seemed likeable and as is the case with children of that age, were anxious to get on with their activities, so were on their way.

Looking at the children as they departed, the wife commented on the fact that she did not see them nearly enough and that they were growing to adulthood before her almost in a blink of the eye. The husband, at this point, indicated his agreement with his wife's desire to spend more time with the children before they grew up. He interestingly added, as did his father previously, that it seemed that one day he and his wife woke up and suddenly needed two salaries. Again, the "invisible hand" of government, with its need for more and more money, necessitated two members of the family working. They indicated how things were in the past and how they wished it were possible to return; however those things that were luxuries in the past now became necessities.

The wanderer observed that this mysterious transition from luxuries to necessities was not all that mysterious; it was the legislators behind the walls of the grand palace planning this transition so that their own wealth and power would increase. The wanderer did not want to monopolize most of this "day of grace" for the family, so he made his exit and they mutually agreed that they would meet again.

As he left the home, he thought to himself that this growing disconnection between the parents and children must have some sort of effect on family life. Certain foreboding thoughts came to his mind. What was happening to the relationship between husband and wife as they passed each other from home to work? If the parents weren't home at those critical times when the children needed their advice and guidance, where would the children turn? What was happening to those special moments when the family got together as a unit and shared experiences? How were family responsibilities restructured from that time when there was a traditional rhythm of family life? This and many such questions turned inside his head as he pondered how forces outside this changing family structure were affecting and changing the family life.

Chapter V

he next morning over breakfast with the elderly citizen, which had now become a daily ritual, the elderly citizen asked him what he thought about the meeting with his family the day before. The wanderer responded by mentioning that he was struck at how much the family was affected by forces outside it. The elderly citizen pondered the thought and decided to introduce him to the superintendent of his grandchildren's school, with whom he occasionally had breakfast, and who lived across the street from the inn. As it happened, this was one of the weeks when the school was closed for the holidays and the elderly citizen said that he would invite the school superintendent to breakfast the next morning. The wanderer thanked the elderly citizen as he left and couldn't help thinking to himself how nice it was that this citizen was so helpful in guiding him through his journey of discovery.

The next morning, as usual, he met the elderly citizen for breakfast, and with him was the superintendent of schools. He was a middle-aged man with a stressed presence and was sympathetic to the youth of this generation because he had experienced things as they were before this sea change in the village. As they were eating breakfast, he mentioned that it was such a relief to be out of the school system for a week. He said that he had never felt that emotion in past years, but with the current problems, it was becoming more and more stressful running the school system. At this point, the wanderer asked him if he wo uld elaborate on the current stressful situation. He began by indicating that all forms of parental discipline seemed to be falling apart. In the past, parents would send a well-disciplined student to school, and the school simply had to educate, which w as their role. Today, both parents are working, and in divorced families, only one parent is at home (he would later discuss with us the high divorce rate in recent years). Children's behavior and home discipline were breaking down, and the results were children being dropped off at school with multiple discipline problems. Since they were paying such high taxes, parents expected the teachers to solve these problems, while at the same time educating this new generation of undisciplined children. His impression was that the whole system was breaking down. Asked to further elaborate on this apparently deteriorating situation, he almost seemed relieved to get this weighty problem out to an interested party.

In the past, he said, children came to school prepared to learn. The children had traditional two-parent families where they were trained in a supervised atmosphere, which logically led to that time when the school program for learning was the next step in their development. The parents, at least one of whom was always there when the child returned from school, reinforced the schooling process to ensure that the learning which was imparted at school was further developed at home through homework and family discussions. Now this mutually reinforcing connection had been broken because many families had both parents working and the child returned to an empty home without the adult guidance required to complete the circle of learning and socialization. When they did return home, parents were failing to teach discipline because they were either too tired after a long day of work, or did not want to spend the precious little time together arguing, so they gave in to the children, in part from guilt.

The wanderer was beginning to see the possible ramifications of this disconnect between school and home and its potential for familial disruption. In the morning a child was going to school not well prepared to learn because of the unsupervised home life, and in the evening the child was leaving school and entering an empty home where there was no supervised program to follow. At this stage of development, when a child is learning social behavior without adult supervision, the results could be disruptive to both the child's socialization and education.

As if he heard what the wanderer was thinking, the superintendent said that it might be productive for him to hear about this disconnect and its ramifications from an adolescent's point of view. Since this was a holiday period, he suggested that he meet his neighbors' child, who was a student at his school. This student, although a product of two working parents, seemed, according to the superintendent, to be one of the better-adjusted and intelligent students and might be able to give some valuable input to our discussion. With this agreed upon, we ended our breakfast dialogue and would meet the next morning.

The morning meetings were becoming an educational process for the wanderer and this morning's meeting was quite a round table discussion with the wanderer, the elderly citizen, the school superintendent, and the student in attendance. The centerpiece of this meeting would be the perspective of the young student, so obviously attention was centered on him. His perspective was unique in that he had never, during his short life, been directly acquainted with the traditional two-parent family home. He was obviously aware of the traditional family through his discussions with adults and those few students who still maintained this traditional family group, so he did have a comparative point of view. The superintendent had informed him of this meeting's topic, so he had personal perspectives to initiate the discussion. First he noted that many of his friends were in newly divorced family situations. Through discussions with his friends, he believed that the increasing divorce rate was due in large part to the fact that both parents were working and this impacted their relationship in two ways. First, they were losing contact with each other since they were seeing each other less and less as they passed each other on the way to and from work, and that time they previously spent together bonding their relationship was disappearing. Second, each parent was beginning to participate in workplace activities separate from and outside the family. His impression from his friends was that it was neither party's fault, but the nature of this changed relationship. The casualty of this major change was not only the husband and wife, but also the children involved. He noted the children, in turn, were beginning to develop their own new social life in response to the changing relationship between their parents. No longer could they rely on family activities, as was the case in the past. They now had to create new activities based around their peers.

The group repeated the theme of this family disconnect and the wanderer was hard pressed to see any benefits of this new lifestyle. If the intact family unit was the goal, as was the case in the past, it seemed to have disastrous results. If the two working parents were at the center of this familial disconnect, the wanderer decided to revisit the reason for this new arrangement to see if there were forces beyond the greed and shortsightedness of the legislators who were responsi ble for this current state of affairs.

As he entered the inn.... The atmosphere was quite informal....Unlike their formal visage at the palace, the legislators...seemed to have a very casual presence....

Chapter VI

hen he last visited the palace to view the legislative process, he noticed that between sessions many of the legislators gathered at a local inn outside the palace grounds. According to a citizen to whom he spoke, this was an historic meeting place for the legislators and allowed them to unwind from the, at times, rigors of the legislative meetings. He decided that this might be the place where he could gather some important impressions from the legislative point of view.

The next morning he decided to visit the inn outside the palace to see if he could informally discuss with the legislators some of the issues he had been discussing with the local citizens. As he entered the inn, it was fairly early in the morning, and there were few legislators there. The atmosphere was quite informal, not unlike the inn where he had been discussing matters with the citizens. Unlike their formal visage at the palace, the legislators, few as there were, seemed to have a very casual presence, which made it easy for him to sit at one table with a stately looking gentleman who was enjoying his morning repast. The wanderer introduced himself and asked if he might join him. The elderly gentleman was surprisingly friendly and did not at all mind if he joined him.

The wanderer began the conversation by asking the gentleman if he were a legislator since it was his understanding that this was a meeting place for many of the legislators. The stately looking gentleman said that he was indeed a legislator. With this opening to the dialogue, the wanderer said that he had been attending the legislative meetings for the past several weeks and was fascinated by the process and had several questions that had crossed his mind and wondered if the legislator would mind enlightening him regarding these questions. The legislator not only assented, but also encouraged the wanderer to continue his questioning process.

The wanderer began by indicating that at all of the sessions he had been attending, the concerns seemed to involve monies to be spent on existing programs or new expenditures. Even if the discussion was not about increasing tax monies, it might be about reducing the size of increases rather than actually decreasing spending. As he was commenting on the process, the wanderer was careful not to directly offend the legislator while at the same time not avoid the critical issue of increasing revenues imposed on the citizenry. The legislator, who had been noting with interest all of the wanderer's remarks, was used to this kind of cross-examination from not only his adversarial legislators, but also the citizens whom he represented. Without hesitation, he began his part of the dialogue with very specific examples. First, he said, he was the chairman of the legislative committee concerned with immigration into the country. He noted that, in past years, immigrants entering the country had to be vouched for and supported, if necessary, by their sponsors. New immigrants coming into the country had to be self-sufficient and not rely on governmental assistance, or be deported. In recent years, the governmental policy had changed. Under the new immigration laws, immigrants coming into the country could immediately go into subsidized governmental programs which would pay for health insurance, housing, food, and medical care. Since these were government programs, the citizens paid for these services through new taxes. The result of this new policy (and he did not know how or when these programs were initiated, but that they seemed to be in place and working overnight) was effecting the government and citizens on several levels. First, taxes had to be increased to pay for these services. Second, bureaucracies had to be created to manage these programs, which increased the tax requirements further. It became clear to the wanderer that on this one level there could be an enormous increase in the size of government. From the outside, growth in government seemed to be easy to halt, or at least reduce, but as he began to see how the government was increasing, the solution to decreasing the size seemed to be a more complex task.

The wanderer had taken quite a bit of time from the legislator merely to address this one aspect of the governmental growth problem, and he had many questions that still circulated in his head, but knew that the legislator had to leave for his responsibilities at the palace. He thanked him and asked if he would be imposing on the legislator if he could further discuss these problems. The legislator seemed very happy in terms of the feedback he was getting from the wanderer, and also seemed to enjoy his company, so he agreed to meet at another time.

Chapter VII

he meeting gave him some valuable insight into the interplay between the citizens and the government. Prior to his recent meeting with the legislator, his assumption was that this huge bureaucracy was the single villain in this "theatre," however the picture was now a bit more complex. The line between the government and the citizens was becoming a little less clear. There were various channels he could explore to further his investigation. He thought that a productive area to begin might be to talk to a new immigrant, since his recent meeting with the legislator illuminated this problem and an immigrant's perspective might further clarify his most recent revelation.

The next morning he arose and went to the dining room of the inn where he was residing and sat down with his now old friend, the citizen who had introduced him to the several other citizens to whom he had been speaking. The citizen asked him how his investigation was progressing and the wanderer took a good part of the morning updating him on his educational process. When he mentioned that it might be additionally revealing to the interplay between the government and citizens to discuss this multifaceted problem from the point of view of a newly arrived immigrant, the elderly citizen perked up and revealed that one of his newly acquired friends was the father of an immigrant family with whom he enjoyed weekend fishing, a pastime which the y both shared. As was the case in the past, he suggested that they meet the following morning at the inn for breakfast.

As he arose the next morning, there was a knock on his door. Upon opening it, he was surprised to see his elderly citizen friend. He greeted him and queried him as to the reason for his presence. The elderly citizen responded by telling him that his immigrant friend wondered if he would join them for breakfast at their home, since his wife could not leave the home due to her obligation to care for their children. Apparently she had learned of their meeting, and she and her older son were interested in meeting him. The wanderer enthusiastically answered in the positive since he felt that if he could get the entire family's view it would be very productive. He asked if the visitor would object to sitting in his reception room while he finished dressing.

Shortly they left the inn and headed down the road until they reached a large development which, unlike the surrounding single-family homes, was apparently a community complex that housed various families. As they approached, the elderly citizen noted that this was a government owned public housing facility. It had been constructed in recent years to accommodate the new influx of immigrants and had been full from almost the day it was built, according to the elderly citizen.

As they neared the complex, the citizens whom they passed were more diverse in skin color and dress than those citizens whom he had met in his limited exposure to date. As they entered the main lobby, in addition to the diversity of citizens, he became aware of an aroma in the air, an unusual essence that, as he was to discover later, was the result of the exotic elements of the meals which were prepared daily.

They knocked on the door of the immigrant family's home and as they entered, again the exotic aroma of the food. This last influx of immigrants was of a dark and swarthy nature, and he assumed that they were from one of the eastern kingdoms. The recent flood of immigrants into this kingdom was due, in part, to the higher standard of living and the atmosphere of freedom that was evidently lacking in the kingdom they were leaving.

The greeting was quite warm, probably because the father knew the wanderer, at lea st indirectly, since the immigrant and the wanderer's citizen friend shared weekend fishing activities.

The great contrast in cultures was evident immediately. As he glanced around the room, he was not only impressed by the differences in the darker skin of the immigrants and the exotic aroma of the food, but by the furnishings which they had obviously brought with them from their kingdom. The wife, being a first generation immigrant, wore garb that was foreign to this kingdom; however the son's attire reflected an assimilation of this culture, probably through his associations at the school and his young and impressionable age. The wanderer surmised that the next generation would present an entirely assimilated presence. The wife offered him a cup of tea with a pastry that he did not recognize.

Even the tea had an exotic and pleasant taste. The immigrants had been in the kingdom long enough so they could understand and speak the language adequately, at least to the two visitors.

The wanderer asked the husband what he did to support his family. The immigrant responded that he had a part-time job helping in the kitchen at the inn. He further indicated that the position was less than he felt he was qualified to do, but with his limited use of the language and his exotic presence, it was the best he was able to procure at this time. He added that it was next to impossible to support the family with his limited income. The wanderer asked him if he considered having his wife work to supplement their income. The immigrant replied that it would not be proper for his wife to leave the children at home without parental supervision. In addition, there were many government sponsored supplementary income sources that were available to low-income families. He believed that the choice to use these resources was a far better option than to deprive his children of their mother's supervision while they were in their early youth. How ironic, the wanderer thought to himself. On the one hand, citizens born in this kingdom have opted, or have been forced into deciding, to have both parents work to support an ever-increasing upward style of living. On the other hand, the immigrant family had decided that the family value of having at least one of the parents remain in the home to care for the children was most important. Of course the option of government subsidy because of their low income was not currently available to the main body of citizens due to their higher income. The result of these juxtaposed positions seemed to favor the choice of the immigrants, at least on the level of family values. The main body of citizens had more material accumulations and a higher standard of living, if measured on an economic level. The immigrant family was more intact in terms of family, but they relied heavily on governmental subsidies that were paid for by the main body of tax-paying citizens. This seeming contradiction was further complicated as the wife continued the dialogue by indicating that many of her immigrant friends were not married, but were having children because they knew that the system would support their lifestyle with generous subsidies of housing, food, and cash allowances that would increase as the immigrants had more children. Again, how ironic it was that the government was supporting a program that rewarded unwed mothers to have more children, to the detriment of the taxpayer.

The wanderer was overwhelmed by this wealth of information from the immigrant family. His head was so full of thoughts concerning these new revelations that he needed time to digest the information and decide where he should next direct his energies. He thanked the immigrant family, wished them well, and departed from the complex with his citizen friend.

Chapter VIII

s he sat in his room, so many questions had arisen as a result of his meeting with the immigrant family that he decided that a second meeting with the legislator with whom he had breakfast the other morning would be in order. He wanted to explore answers to the variety of new questions that had emerged as a result of his thought-provoking meeting with the immigrant family.

He suspected that the legislator, as part of his daily routine, would have his breakfast at the inn and, as they discussed at their last breakfast meeting, decided to appear early that morning to continue his discussion. As he entered the inn there was the legislator, as predicted, sitting at the same table having his morning repast. He approached the legislator and was greeted like an old friend. The legislator, with a smile on his face, said that he knew that they would have at least another breakfast meeting to further discuss the many unanswered questions that had been raised at their last meeting. The wanderer updated him on his visit to the immigrant family's home and the many questions that had arisen as a result of that meeting. The elderly legislator knew how complex the problems of the kingdom were and took an interest in the wanderer's quest to explore these tantalizing questions. In addition, it gave him a chance to respond to these apparent contradictions and perhaps shed some light, with his knowledge of these problems, on the subject. The legislator began the discussion by telling the wanderer that an amendment was being brought up in today's legislative session to vote on a petition by a group of liberal legislators to subsidize not only the immigrant family, but also their extended family that they might bring into the kingdom. The wanderer, after the revelations at his meeti ng yesterday with the immigrant family, was so astonished that his mouth was open and he took a few seconds to gather himself and respond. If the tax burden was increasing so precipitously due to the current subsidizing of immigrants, how could they possibly pass new legislation to further burden the citizens? With understanding and sympathy, the legislator smiled and responded by indicating to the astonished wanderer that those legislators who supported this petition represented areas of the kingdom where this immigrant population resided. The existing immigrant population in the area, who represented votes, was pressuring them. Also, internally the huge new bureaucracy that was managing these programs was pressuring them because of an insatiable desire to expand its power and influence, which accompanied the larger size of this leviathan. It was astonishing to the wanderer to hear a legislator, who seemed to be conservative in his views, explain in such a logical manner the rationale of the liberal legislators who supported this next step, in what would appear to be enormous growth of bureaucracy and its accompanying further tax burden on the citizens.

The wanderer thought to himself at what point the tax burden on the citizens would become unbearable. The inevitable direction of the equation seemed obvious. The latest wave of immigrants was not generally self-sufficient in that they could not earn enough to pay their share of taxes. But more troublesome was the fact that the legislators were allowing an ever-increasing proportion of taxes to be used for subsidizing these immigrants. The result seemed obvious to the wanderer. At some point in the equation, the ever-increasing taxes to pay for benefits for the non-contributing immigrants would exceed the permanent citizens' ability to pay for these benefits. Was someone or some legislative body looking at a long-range solution to this problem? Or were current considerations, political and other, making it impossible for them to evaluate this impending collision with enough intensity to avert disaster?

The wanderer brought this perplexing and possibly disastrous scenario to the legislator's attention. He responded by indicating that the legislators as a whole were an informed and intelligent body and certainly were aware of this possible direction. They were, in fact, discussing the long-term possible ramifications of this problem; however, their daily agenda and need to solve current problems did not allow them adequate time to fully address this longer-term problem.

As he looked at the legislator, he began to see a larger possible societal problem — the actual long-term survival of the kingdom. If the current problems were so time-consuming for the legislative body and growing more complex with passing time, even if there was a body of citizens who saw and understood this growing problem and its ramifications, how could they convince the legislative body of the importance of this larger long-term problem and the need to address it now rather than consider it on a more philosophic level? Was a solution possible? A second and possibly more sinister element was the enlightened self-interest of the citizens in general and this legislative body. Was the ordinary citizen so busy with his daily existence and working so hard to keep up with bettering his lifestyle and paying ever-increasing taxes that it was impossible for him to adequately address the problem by pressuring his legislators? Even more alarming was the view from the legislative body. With this ever-growing government and all of its complications, were the legislators a large part of the problem? They were responsible, in large part, for this larger government and were becoming accustomed to the trappings of managing this large bureaucracy, namely wealth and power. Was it possible that the ordinary citizens and the legislators were more concerned with themselves, rather than the well-being of the kingdom, because it might require downsizing their personal lifestyles to avert an oncoming societal disaster?

Both were finishing their breakfast, and he had taken up a good portion of time with the legislator, who would have to return to his task of doing the public business of the kingdom. He detected an expression on the legislator's visage that gave him the impression that he had opened doors that were both challenging and worrisome to the legislator. No longer were their meetings a casual encounter discussing matters of a lighter and more general nature. They had become more penetrating and challenging and perhaps disturbing to the legislator. They shook hands, and although the legislator did not offer another invitation to breakfast, did not close the door on such a meeting. The wanderer felt sure that should the occasion arise, he would not be rebuffed should he appear for a future early morning encounter.

From his window at the inn, he could see in the distance a large complex of buildings....it was the kingdom's university of higher learning and was the residence for many of its most learned philosophers.

Chapter IX

s he returned to the inn, many thoughts were spinning around in his head. The kingdom was in a troubled state and its citizens didn't seem to be able to either recognize the seriousness of the problem or have a realistic strategy to establish some sort of normalcy and stability. If his interpretation of the many meetings he had with people was correct, was there any place in the kingdom where these problems were being addressed in a meaningful manner?

From his window at the inn, he could see in the distance a large complex of buildings with a cathedral-type edifice at the center. In recent days he had asked at the inn as to the nature of the complex. He was told that it was the kingdom's university of higher learning and was the residence for many of its most learned philosophers. What an exciting opportunity for him to visit the university to explore how the academic community viewed some of the societal problems that he observed.

Early the next morning, he decided to visit the university to see if in fact the academic community, where theories of government were explored, was addressing the current state of affairs in the kingdom.

The road to the university grounds was a healthy distance, so he had a chance during his walk to meet several of the students who were also on the way to the university. His discussions were short and general in nature, and he did not discuss in depth any particular subjects; however, he made two general observations. First was the general misuse of the language and lack of formal grammatical construction used by the students in their discussions with him. Second and more disturbing was a general profanity that pervaded the discussions. He was aware that this was a small sampling of the student body and would withhold his evaluation until he further delved into this phenomenon. He would have to evaluate if this was a passing rebellious phase of the students as they evolved from their juvenile stage to adulthood, or a more general lifestyle change being developed by the students. On a positive note, one of the students mentioned the name of a professor teaching one of his courses who was concerned with the interface between academia and the general affairs of the kingdom. This particular professor discussed on a regular basis as part of their classroom activities many specific applications of their classroom theories as they affected the overall functioning of the kingdom. How lucky he felt that through this encounter with the student he might introduce himself to the professor and hopefully shed some light on his ongoing investigation.

As they approached the university, the students went their separate ways as they headed to their specific classroom assignments. The wanderer went about his task of attempting to locate this professor whom he would try to engage in a discussion to further elevate his knowledge of this connection between the university and the rest of the kingdom.

Upon entering the main entrance to the university, his eyes were brought to the attention of a large open area with a busy population of professional-looking citizens. The sign above the opening to this area was worded "Administrative Offices." "Aha!" he said to himself. This is where he would begin his search for the professor whom he hoped would help him with answers to the multitude of questions that were keeping his mind in a state of anxiety. He approached the front desk of a pleasant-looking middle-aged lady who asked if she could be of assistance. Her plea sant demeanor and calm presence made it easy for him to query her about the whereabouts of the professor in question. Without hesitation she recognized the name of the professor and referred to her log to see if she could locate the professor and identify his schedule for the day. She opened the log to the appropriate page and told the wanderer that he was fortunate, since the professor had no classes this morning and would likely be in his office updating his backlog of paperwork. She assured the wander er that paperwork was a major chore for the popular professor and that this was the time when she would schedule students and other visitors to see the busy professor, since at just about any other time he would either be teaching his heavily attended courses at the university or traveling on his never-ending lecture tours.

Following the directions from the pleasant lady at the front desk, he walked down the long hall from the administration area until he reached an area of inner offices. He opened the door and, as she described, the professor's office with his name on the door was the first office he encountered. The pleasant lady had apparently called the professor to advise him that he should expect a visitor, for when the wanderer knocked, the professor was at the door to greet him. He had expectations of encountering an elderly, bespectacled, scholarly-appearing individual, but instead the professor had a more boyish and athletic visage with a slight graying at the temples and a wiry frame. How appearances can deceive us, as he was to learn. The professor was apparently accustomed to being interviewed, for after they greeted each other, the professor offered the wanderer a cup of tea. This gesture put the wanderer at ease, and it facilitated a beginning to their discussion. The wanderer started the discussion with the question of how long the professor had been employed by the university. This initial question opened the door for the professor to expand his answer to a brief history of his career at the university, from his early days as a student, his eventual entrance and completion of graduate school, and his present position which included lecture tours and several sabbaticals that added to his proficiency and expertise in his field of studies. The wanderer could not help but notice the ease and fluidity with which the young professor described in brief outline form his personal history. Was it any wonder that he was such a popular force with the students at the university? The most appropriate subject to start with seemed to be his encounter with the students whom he met on his way to the university. As he described in detail the encounters with the students, emphasizing their misuse of the language and the general profanity, the professor gave him a knowing smile. He began his response by indicating that not that many years ago when he was a student, the rebelliousness was also present, but that this generation, in his opinion, was much more intense and detached from the establishment. In fact, he agreed with the wanderer that he perceived a more pervasive movement than the rebelliousness he had mentioned earlier. The movement appeared to be more than the juvenile rejection of authority of earlier years. He indicated that one of the main causes, and there were many, was the breakdown of discipline in the home. He was well aware of the parents' absence at home to supervise and lead the youth. He emphasized that students came to class without the basic rules of behavior, which should be learned at home. How could teachers, whose role was to educate, be expected to not only teach these undisciplined youth, but also discipline them, which was the role of the parents? The wanderer was not only reflecting on this statement, but also reviewing i n his mind some of the same observations that were present in his earlier discussions with other citizens.

The barriers being removed, the wanderer expanded his discussion to one of the problems of recent immigration policy and its social and economic effects on the kingdom. The wanderer noticed a mildly strained presence on the professor as he addressed the problem. The professor informed him that he himself was from an immigrant family, although he was born in this kingdom. The wanderer was to later learn that even though he was from an immigrant family, the professor would agree with most of the wanderer's positions on the problems under discussion. The professor maneuvered to a more pressing problem for him personally, indicating that many of the students arriving at the university brought with them prior learning problems, which were probably present in the home before they even began school. In short, he indicated that if the parents did not properly address the problems prior to the children attending early school, the problems would only be further exacerbated as they progressed through the higher learning process. The wanderer thought to himself that if, in fact, what the professor and those citizens to whom he spoke earlier said was true, was this downward evolution of values becoming the norm? Was this a harbinger of the future leadership in the kingdom? What a challenging and perplexing position for the professor and his colleagues to be facing.

Both the wanderer and professor seemed drained of energy at this point, but the intense discussion interested the professor. Although he had other pressing duties to address, he invited the wanderer to visit with him and his wife at their home the following weekend where they could continue their discussion in a more relaxed atmosphere with no time constraints.

For the next few days prior to his meeting with the professor at his home, the wanderer took daily trips to the university where he could discuss university life, on an informal basis, with both students and university employees. Interestingly, the views of the employees at the university differed substantially in many areas from those views held by the students. The university employees in general thought that the students were a spoiled and pampered group of youths, discipline in general was too lax, and university rules were not enforced strenuously enough. Pressure by the student body and their parents seemed too prevalent in influencing university policy. The rules of performance were so compromised that the credibility of a university education and degree were at best marginal. From the point of view of the students, which was not unusual for students, this was a period of exploration and the rules should be challenged. The dilemma for the wanderer in speaking to both groups was who had a better grasp of the truth. Again, these were general impressions and would help in his evaluation when he met that weekend with the professor at his home.

Chapter X

hat Saturday was a bright and sunny morning, and the wanderer looked forward to his brisk walk to the university and his hopefully revealing discussion with the popular professor. As he approached the university, there was a group of ivy-covered buildings to the left of the main entrance. Following his directions from the professor, the wanderer entered the complex, which led to the building that housed the majority of professors at the university. He was surprised to see that the quarters were quite luxurious and manicured gardens s urrounded the complex. He assumed that since the quarters were this luxurious, the professors were held in high esteem. As he was to learn later, the professors were indeed held in high esteem and not only were they highly remunerated, but the university subsidized their quarters. These factors would contribute considerably to his later evaluation of the professor's opinions. He knocked on the door of the professor's luxurious quarters and was greeted by his wife, who was not only gracious in appearance, but gave the wanderer a warm and intimate introduction to their home. It was dominated by a series of bookcases and shelves filled with many books covering a multitude of subjects, some of which were not even related to his field of expertise. The home was filled with exotic and expensive furniture and furnishings, which indicated that they had eclectic taste. In addition, it appeared that the professor was a renaissance person with many interests and expensive tastes. The wife directed the wanderer to the study where he was greeted by the professor. In his casual attire he looked even more boyish than at their more formal meeting several days earlier. In addition to his casual appearance, today he had a much calmer presence, partly because he was in his home with no outside interference, unlike at his university office. He was reading a student's term paper, and remarked that he had written better papers in his pre-university days. He was obviously anxious to discuss some of the matters left unaddressed at his office. The professor noted that the current university standards had been lowered considerably in the past few years. It seemed that the authorities dictating the kingdom's higher educational policy determined that all students today should have the opportunity for a university education, with little emphasis on qualifications. His concerns were on two levels. First, the university administration was pressuring the professors to be more "cooperative" in grading the students. Second, and more far reaching, would be the effect on the kingdom as the students matriculated and entered the economy. If these students were less qualified, how would this affect the future leadership and management of the kingdom? Even more sinister, if the kingdom was overwhelmed with these minimally educated university students, and there was only a fixed number of openings available for university level positions, there would be more and more minimally educated university graduates with fewer and fewer professional positions available. The result would inevitably be frustrated graduates accepting positions that did not require a university education. The wanderer thought to himself, again, how ironic. On the one hand, less than adequately educated students who thought that they were bona fide graduates would be applying for positions that they were probably unable to handle. On the other hand, since those types of positions were not available, they would be settling for lesser jobs that did not require a university education. The result would be an unhappy and discontented work force that would add frustration to a large segment of the kingdom. The professor had serious reservations regarding this current trend in education. He commented that all students sh ould not be granted the opportunity for a university education. It was not that he was offering an elitist program for education, he stated, but that there were many positions in the kingdom that did not require a university education and these duties had to be carried out by someone. His theory seemed logical; however, the wanderer noted in his comportment and explanation an attitude that gave the appearance of superiority. The wanderer would have to give this interpretation further thought.

While the wanderer was pondering this explanation, the professor decided to pursue the immigration topic that they had begun the other day. The professor seemed rather bitter about this current wave of immigrants. He reiterated the thought expressed previously to the wanderer by other citizens regarding reliance on the government for support, rather than being personally responsible. Again, the more citizens to whom he spoke, the more this was a recurring theme, leading the wanderer to believe that this was a valid claim.

The professor continued and set forth a theory that he believed would stem the tide of the current immigration problem and help stabilize the kingdom. His belief was that only immigrants who could contribute some asset, either intellectually or with a specific skill, should be allowed to enter the kingdom. He cited the history of the development of the kingdom, noting that in the last great wave of immigration, the kingdom was young and undeveloped and could utilize all of the incoming immigrants, including those with minimal, if any, skills. The situation today was different. The kingdom was fully developed and had no need for new immigrants without skills or assets, since the internal work force was adequate to manage the affairs of the kingdom. Only new immigrants who had specific skills or wealth to help grow the kingdom to the next level were required. This new immigrant who was educated with specific skills would not be a burden to the taxpayer, indeed, he would add to the tax base. Under the current situation, where most of the new immigrants were living mainly on governmental subsidy, they were surely an added burden to the current citizens.

The wanderer could not refute the logic of the professor's argument; however, his earlier impression of the leaning towards elitism was resurfacing. Without ascribing a positive or negative evaluation to the professor's position, the wanderer noted that all of the citizens expressed a position based primarily on their own self-interest. Again, this was not so much a critique of the individual citizen, but possibly a natural proclivity of all citizens, for after all, wasn't society a man-made vehicle for the survival of all individuals? It would follow, the wanderer speculated, that each individual participated in the structure based primarily on his self-interest. All of those societal decisions he made were rationalized to satisfy the individual citizen's needs and how they related to his survival and well-being.

As the wanderer pondered these thoughts, the professor's wife, at just the appropriate pause in the discussion, suggested a light luncheon break. The meal, as was the case with their lifestyle, was both elegant and gracious, and their discussion during the repast was kept light and entertaining. The wanderer thought to himself how pleasant was his visit and hoped that they could enjoy each other's company at another time. As if he heard the wanderer's very thoughts, the professor indicated that he was a member of a committee that oversaw military affairs in the kingdom and a few select observers were allowed to attend the meetings. He suggested that by accompanying him to the meeting he might see the affairs of the kingdom in a broader context. Without seeming overly anxious, the wande rer agreed to attend the meeting, which was to take place within a few days. Time had sped by and as he left, the wanderer not only promised to attend the meeting with the professor, but also agreed to meet again at his home.

Behind the elevated platform was the large flag of the kingdom. The walls...were covered with various maps of the provinces of the kingdom....How could the wanderer not be impressed?

Chapter XI

he morning of the meeting of the committee on military affairs turned out to be dark and gray, with a gusty easterly chilling wind. Might this be a harbinger of the upcoming meeting? The committee on military affairs met monthly in a large chamber in the west wing of the palace. He entered the palace grounds as he had on many occasions during his visits to the legislative sessions. As he approached the palace, he was directed to the west wing. At the entrance, he was met by members of the palace guard who confronted the wanderer as he neared. These members of the guard had a more seri ous presence than those at the main entrance to the palace grounds, and challenged the wanderer to identify himself. Fortunately for the wanderer, the guard had been informed in advance of his attendance at the meeting, and upon identifying himself, was a llowed to enter the chamber. Inside, the chamber impressed the wanderer. At the far end of the hall was an elevated platform with a long bench and chairs to seat the chairmen who headed the committee. Behind the elevated platform was the large flag of the kingdom. The walls to the back of the

platform were covered with various maps of the provinces of the kingdom. In the middle of the chamber was a splendid chandelier, which illuminated the large portraits on the walls of what appeared to be the milita ry leaders of the kingdom, both past and present. How could the wanderer not be impressed?

As the members of the committee filed in, the various military uniforms were overwhelmingly noticeable and the authoritarian presence of the military was soon felt as the meeting was called to order. Unlike the legislative meetings he had attended earlier, with the give and take of the various legislators, that attitude was not present at this meeting. The agenda was quite rigid, as might be expected at a military meeting. Although there was a sprinkling of non-military citizens on the committee, including legislators and other professionals like his friend the professor, the dominance of the military was, to say the least, pronounced. The agenda for this day's meeting was internal affairs of the kingdom. First to be discussed was the developing immigration problem. The speaker addressing this problem was a middle-aged officer of the guard. The splendor of his uniform was surpassed only by the multitude of medal s he wore, indicating his participation in many campaigns. In keeping with his appearance, his presentation was both forceful and elegant in discussing the problem. He began by stressing the seriousness of the problem in recent times and the urgent need to address the problem forthright before it got out of control. Specifically, the new immigrant groups, unlike previous immigrants, were not assimilating to the common culture of the kingdom. Rather, they were importing their own cultures and competing with the kingdom's culture. A multi-cultural base was developing. Rather than primary allegiance to the kingdom, each culture was developing an allegiance to that culture first, after which it would accede to the rules of the kingdom. This, the kingdom could not allow. In previous generations, new immigrants, although retaining their culture, adopted the culture of the kingdom. At the same time that they respected their own culture, the immigrants understood that it was second to the culture of the kingdom. If this new multiculturalism was allowed to continue, the kingdom could eventually crumble due to the dissipation of the central rule. The officer's argument was both compelling and logical. The wanderer could envision possible ominous implications to the solution of these problems, and if the solution involved draconian measures, the stability of the kingdom might be challenged. As he left the podium, many of the chairmen congratulated the officer for his performance.

The next to appear was a surprise to the wanderer, for she was a young, high-ranking officer with darker skin whom the wanderer was to later learn was the daughter of an immigrant family from one of the eastern kingdoms. She had an impressive visage in her military attire, having multiple medals on her spotless uniform, as did her predecessor, and carrying herself quite erect as would be expected of a military officer. Her responsibility in the affairs of the kingdom was its stability and well-being. To this point she began her presentation, with a critical analysis of the growing immigration policy, which encouraged public subsidy of the new immigrants. Her involvement with the fiscal affairs committee revealed the alarming increase in taxes as a percentage of the citizens' income. She related this increase in large part to the increasing subsidy, on many levels, of the new immigrants. She speculated to the committee for a moment, on the theoretical level, that she assumed that some administrative body above this committee had developed a strategy to monitor the percentage of income that the citizens would tolerate for taxes. She continued and speculated that the citizens would tolerate paying a percentage of their wages for taxes to maintain the kingdom; however, when the taxes rose beyond this percentage, she assumed that the citizens would refuse to pay their taxes. At this point, a system of enforcement above and beyond the current one might be required, or the system might, in fact, become dysfunctional and be at risk of (and she chose her words carefully) revolution! The committee sat in stunned silence for a moment, for no one apparently had taken the equation this far in evaluating the current accelerated tax increases.

This speech by the young officer proved to be the high point of the meeting and ignited many small conferences upon conclusion of the formal meeting. The wanderer, also stunned by the presentation of the young officer, left the chamber and wondered if, in fact, any body of administrators or legislators abov e this committee was evaluating this problem. By the response of the committee, it didn't appear that this was the case, at least to that depth posed by the young officer. Ominous indeed was her presentation.

Chapter XII

At his evening repast at the inn, he thought deeply about the seriousness of the topics discussed at the military affairs meeting that day and the presentations of the two officers, with the ominous implications weighing heavily on his mind. Upon finishing his meal, he withdrew to his room and although he was exhausted from the day's activities, he had a difficult time in his attempt to sleep. He was quite restless and found himself waking several times during the night. During one of these waking periods, he recalled a passing moment after the meeting when the professor strongly suggested that he attend the meeting again the next day. He indicated, with his knowing smile, that the wanderer might be exposed to additional information that would broaden his horizon even further into the workings of this important committee and its impact on the kingdom.

The morning finally arrived and despite his lack of sleep the previous night, the wanderer found himself looking forward to attending his second day at the meeting. He left the inn at an early hour so he might find a favorable seat in the chamber where he could best view the participants. As he approached the guards at the chamber, their attitude was less challenging than the previous day, and they greeted the wanderer and simply asked for his identification. His early arrival did indeed allow him to position himself close to the podium, thus allowing a close and intimate view of the upcoming proceedings. The gallery was quite full as the committee members entered the chamber. Appar ently the information the professor gave him was also given to quite a few other interested citizens, which led the wanderer to believe that this meeting was indeed to be of some substance. The orderly entrance of the committee members was precisely the s ame as their entrance the preceding day. Any citizen in attendance could not overlook the discipline and precision of this committee. The speaker opened the session by indicating that this hearing would address the subject of foreign relations, and specifically to a problem that had been festering for several months with a neighboring kingdom. The kingdom had been at peace for several years prior to this potential outbreak of hostilities on their border and had reached a point where the committee had to design a strategy to solve this problem. To date the response had been on an ad hoc basis, and negotiations had reached an impasse. What had apparently occurred, as the wanderer was to later learn from the professor, was that an ethnic group from the bordering kingdom had reached a stage of overpopulation due to a higher birth rate and much smaller size. The result, over a period of years, slowly added pressure to the citizens of the small kingdom due to overcrowding and lack of economic growth. The consequence was a gradual infiltration of many citizens from the small kingdom, who accepted lower paying jobs and were becoming defectors. The situation was reaching a critical stage at this time because the rulers in the smaller kingdom were claiming that the territory bordering the larger kingdom, which had a sizeable population of their citizens, should be an autonomous region since it was inhabited mainly by their citizens. To this point the rulers of the kingdom had tolerated the informal incursions across their border because it was not considered a threat, and actually helped the local economy because of the inexpensive labor market it supplied. However, now that the foreign rulers were making territorial claims, the kingdom's authority had to be exercised quickly and forcefully to reestablish rigid borders between the kingdoms.

With this formidable task before them, the meeting was called to order and the chairman introduced the main speaker at this session. As he approached the podium, this celebrated speaker had to be the most spectacular witness of those appearing before the committee. He was a large man exhibiting a full head of white hair with a matching white beard. His spectacles gave him an even more convincing authoritarian appearance. He was in full uniform and his collection of medals almost completely covered the front of his uniform and represented his participation in many military campaigns. Yes, this was indeed the chief of staff on the committee and his reputation preceded him. The wanderer noticed that his portrait was one of those adorning the walls of the chamber and the elderly officer was one of the most celebrated military leaders of the kingdom. The wanderer was to learn, upon completion of the speaker's long dissertation, that he was also the most charismatic of the speakers to appear before the committee.

He began his presentation outlining the framework of the current crisis in much detail, indicating precisely those steps that led to the current impasse. His presentation was further enhanced by many detailed maps of the area under discussion, focusing on the specific areas that demanded resolution. Upon completion of this portion of the presentation, he designated, with additional maps, the current military deployment of the troops of both kingdoms and his suggestions as to adjustments needed by his forces to ensure an early and successful completion of the military operation. The wanderer was fascinated by the logical and forceful presentation that would instill confi dence in anyone present at this meeting. It was obvious that he had been in this high profile decision-making position many times in past years, and his confidence in his strategy was obvious to all present. Equally obvious was his pure enjoyment of bein g at the center of one of the most critical situations currently facing the kingdom. Now it was clear why he was held in such high esteem by both his military colleagues and most, if not all, other public figures in the kingdom.

As he continued, he addres sed the political aspects of the confrontation, and his theories were not only surprising to the wanderer, but disturbing. "First," he began, "the kingdom that is challenging the border is much smaller and less advanced than our kingdom. So as not to alienate some of our citizens, we must begin a campaign to characterize the leaders of that kingdom as less than civilized and brutal; in other words, a campaign must be initiated to 'demonize' the enemy. Once this is accomplished, convincing the citizens that this is a righteous cause is much simpler."

The wanderer thought to himself that if an enemy were encroaching upon a territory it seemed logical that merely informing the citizens that the kingdom's border had to be protected in itself was enough justification for the use of force. The chief of staff, however, found it essential to take one further step, which was in fact a large step in "demonizing" the enemy. This step allowed him to use *any* method to resolve the problem, since he was not only dealing with an enemy, but a "demon" enemy. It seemed to the wanderer that this would open the door for any means of resolving the problem, which might include brutalization of the citizens of the other kingdom, and indeed, possible acquisition of the territory of the defeated enemy. The wanderer's theory was augmented when the chief of staff continued by pointing out that "to ensure this current incursion into the kingdom might be obviated in the future, it might be necessary to occupy a portion of the conquered kingdom's territory to prevent such future incursions."

How easily the rationalization process justified what would appear to be a self-serving decision.

The chief of staff was now in his element. As he continued his rationalizations in the name of na tionalism and protection of the kingdom, his lofty rhetoric and his skill and persuasive powers stirred the majority of those in attendance. His rhetorical skills however, possibly disguised a more sinister side to this charismatic chief of staff, and were not lost on a small minority of those in attendance. A skillful charismatic leader in a position of power who, for whatever reason, might use those powers of persuasion to lead the kingdom to decisions with questionable moral ends might, in fact, underm ine the integrity of the kingdom as those ends became known.

As the chief of staff finished his performance, and it was indeed a performance, the energy with which he projected himself and his strategy was exhausting and left him both exhilarated and fatig ued as he wiped his brow. He left the stage and the applause was deafening, save those few who perceived the questionable moral message and the direction in which it might lead the kingdom. The wanderer himself, caught up in the powerful performance of t he chief of staff, remained in his seat for a few long moments until this pause allowed him time to separate his emotional response to the oration from the secondary impact of a possibly more ominous message of a demagogue.

As he left the chamber, there wa s an excitement in the air as he passed many of the legislators still discussing the content of the speech given by the chief of staff. It was obvious to the wanderer that this would initiate a major internal debate among the members of the committee.

During his many visits to the university grounds he could not help but notice at the center of the university complex the cathedral, an awe-inspiring edifice....

Chapter XIII

His walk back to the inn that afternoon was not only long, but he was beginning to comprehend some of the reasons for the uneasiness he felt when he first met with the citizens in the marketplace. The problems were many; and much of the malaise seemed to be caused by the moral integrity, or lack thereof, in the kingdom. If moral deca y appeared to be at the center of the multitude of problems facing the kingdom, where better to further his investigation than at its religious core? To this point his investigation had revealed many troublesome problems. Some of the citizens had given him indications as to the nature of these problems, and even possible solutions to some of them. However, they were only partial and superficial solutions to a problem that was more endemic and threatening to the survival of the kingdom. If the kingdom was to survive, its morality had to be dominant. Should this morality not be intact, then was the kingdom worth saving?

During his many visits to the university grounds he could not help but notice at the center of the university complex the cathedral, an awe-inspiring edifice that had been grandly designed and constructed many years before. The logic to his search inevitably led him to this moral center of the kingdom.

Early the next morning, which happened to be a Sunday, he decided to attend the services at the cathedral to experience first hand what moral message was being imparted to the citizens, and perhaps meet and interview one of the religious leaders who was promulgating his message from the pulpit.

As he neared the cathedral, citizens were entering in small groups. The wanderer, once inside, located a pew toward the rear of the chamber so he might better observe some of the citizens and their reactions to the sermon that morning. His first impression of this house of worship was the artistic detail that predominated. There were intimately detailed statues that almost humanized, yet idealized, those figures representing church history from early times, and a series of artistically detailed and colorful murals on the walls, which further developed the history of the religion. The multi-colored stained glass panels, which permitted the outside light to filter into the cathedral, colorfully accented the interior. The atmosphere reflected a well-organized and strategic plan, orchestrated many years before, to visually and spiritually elevate this sanctuary above and beyond the common existence of its believers.

Once the wanderer was able to digest the grand display of this most holy chamber, his more mundane observations revealed that many of the pews were empty. This surprised the wanderer since this was Sunday, the holy day of worship, and he expected to see the cathedral overflowing with the faithful. In addition, he noted that most of the citizens were elderly, with very few younger citizens in attendance. These two observations led him to the conclusion that the power of the church that might have, at one time, been a dominating force in the kingdom, in recent years had relinquished its position of primacy. He hoped an interview with one of the religious leaders might help to either buttress his opinion, or challenge it, based on facts to which the wanderer might not be privy.

The minister, a gray-haired elderly citizen, from his pulpit high above the faithful appeared to be a fatherly and accepting church leader. This was unexpected to the wanderer, who had envisioned a more powerful and domineering representative of the church. The fatherly minister began his sermon with a scripted presentation, which was apparently part of the religious rh etoric used over many years to establish a reverent tone for his presentation that was to follow. This device, which was more mechanical than inspiring, had apparently functioned over the years, so it became an integral part of the weekly presentation. Once past this mechanical portion of his address, he began his sermon by identifying some of the major problems that the church believed were of concern to the citizens. His identification of those problems was certainly in consonance with many of those pr oblems presented to the wanderer during his travels. The difficulty the wanderer was having with the fatherly minister's presentation was that his critique was more accepting than critical. His message seemed to be that the times were changing, and many of these issues that would have been severely criticized or acted upon in past years, were now being accepted, or at least tolerated, in the name of change.

As the faithful listened to the words of the minister, the wanderer noticed their mechanical response, as though in a stupor. What the wanderer was witnessing at this gathering did not happen overnight, rather it appeared that it was a process that had been festering over many years, and both the minister and his followers seemed almost in a trance. Possibly the passivity and inaction by the rulers in addressing those troublesome problems had infected the citizens, who also seemed helpless to respond to the developing crisis in the kingdom. It certainly did not appear that the church was in a position to stem the tide of decay, for lack of a better word, fomenting in the kingdom. The wanderer felt obligated to at least approach the minister to see if his perception was true, and if so, why the church was unable to play a more active role in defending the moral integrity of the kingdom.

Upon completion of the service, the wanderer visited the minister's quarters, a rather plain attachment to the rear of the cathedral. As was the case with the minister at the sermon, his quarters were similarly unremarkable in appearance. The wanderer knocked on the large wooden door and presently a pleasant appearing lady, who was apparently in the employ of the ministers, opened the door. After a congenial exchange of greetings, he was ushered into the home and asked to wait while the pleasant looking lady departed to fetch the minister.

Several long moments later, the elderly minister hobbled down the stairs to greet the wanderer. At closer examination he looked older and more fragile than he appeared in the pulpit. He gave the wanderer a kind smile, shook his hand, and welcomed him to his home. The wanderer, with deference to the minister's age and frailty, carefully structured his words so as not to upset the minister and thereby possibly attenuate any meaningful dialogue that might take place. The wanderer diplomatically began by complimenting the minister on the splendor of his place of worship and carefully mentioned that he noticed that all of the pews were not filled. He queried the minister if this was normally the case, or was there some reason for the paucity of citizens at the service. Surprisingly, the elderly minister did not need prodding to explain the current state of affairs in terms of attendance at the service; in fact, he expanded his answer to address additional problems currently facing the church. He began the dialogue by indicating that there was a general malaise in the kingdom. The wanderer sat up and gave full attention to the minister, for this was precisely where he hoped the discussi on would lead. As the minister spoke, he miraculously almost appeared younger, as he had been apparently waiting for some time to elaborate on the ills of the kingdom with the proper person to share his thoughts. "This general malaise," he continued, "is due in part to the excesses of materialism in the kingdom. In the past, spiritualism was far more predominant and the role of the church was a major part of family life. Today, citizens are surrounding themselves with many of the material goods available due to the successful economic state of affairs. With both husband and wife working, more money is available to buy more and more of these material goods. The problem is that the more of these luxuries they accumulate, the more these luxuries are becoming necessities, which in turn keeps both husband and wife working to pursue these growing necessities. Obviously," the minister continued, "with the citizens requiring more material goods, their spiritual needs are being pushed into the background. Many citizens are paying lip service to their church because they have less time for their religion.

A secondary and even more insidious factor is now beginning to surface. Between the low attendance at the services by the citizens, and the growing and inviting atmosphere of materialism, fewer recruits are making themselves available to the ministry, opting for more lucrative careers offered in other areas of endeavor. The result," said the minister, "could be devastating for the church. First, with so much emphasis on materialism by the citizens, attendance at the services is declining. Second, with fewer young citizens entering the ministry, the pool of ministers is declining. With mostly older ministers remaining to preach the word, a new interpretation of the scriptures by the younger ministers is not developing, thus making the message to those few younger citizens attending the services less relevant."

The minister's discussion was both moving and believable, unlike his earlier presentation at the chur ch. But behind this compelling presentation, the wanderer detected a fatalism and acceptance of the changing position of the church. The church, the wanderer concluded, would not, in and of itself, be the vehicle around which the kingdom could rally to s tem this decline.

As the wanderer departed, thanking the minister for his valuable time, he observed the minister hobbling back up the stairs, again the aged religious leader he had observed when he first arrived.

Chapter XIV

he next day the wanderer woke to a dark and dreary morning. The weather paralleled his feelings as he reflected on his visit the day before with the minister. He had expected the church, which had been a pillar of stability for the kingdom, at least until recent times, to have some reasonable strategy for righting its ills. Although there were high points in his meeting with the elderly minister, the enlightened vision of a logical and realistic plan for the future survival and well-being of the kingdom was sadly lacking, leaving the wanderer in a quandary as to where to turn. As he pondered this dilemma, his thoughts turned to the professor and his knowing smile, recalling his suggestions of various resources that might provide a more global outlook regarding the ills of the kingdom. The more the wanderer thought about the wisdom of the professor in his selection of those resources, the more he felt that maybe the professor understood his predicament. Rather than relying on his own interpretation, the wanderer might benefit from other enlightened viewpoints, thus allowing him a spectrum of opinions for comparison. Another visit with the professor was in order, and recalling their conversation at his last visit, he remembered that the professor indicated that he would be most happy to meet again. He could usually be found at home on Saturday mornings, either working on his book or attending to paperwork for his students.

Early the following morning, the wanderer was up at the break of dawn. He went downstairs to have a cup of tea before he began his hike to the professor's home. Sitting at a table by himself was the elderly gentleman to whom he had spoken it seemed so long ago. Since that time, he had seen and talked to so many people concerning the state of affairs in the kingdom that his perception of its condition was quite a bit more complex than when they had first spoken. When the elderly citizen queried him as to the status of his inquiry, the wanderer's response was not only more circumspect because of all of his encounters, but probably quite a bit confusing to the elderly citizen, who was a simple man. They exchanged pleasantries, chatted for a few moments, and the wanderer was on his way to see the learned professor.

The hike to the professor's home was long, but invigorating, and gave him time to organize his thoughts into some semblance of a logical format to present to the professor. While he was generating this intellectual exercise in his mind, he wondered if the professor was also organizing a response to his inquiries since the wanderer had, subsequent to their first visit, ascribed much respect for the professor's intuitive and intellectual sense.

As he neared the home, the professor's wife was in the garden tending her flowers. The landscaping was quite exquisitely designed and led the wanderer to reason that not only did his wife have a good sense of design, but also thoroughly enjoyed the labor of maintaining this charming exterior to their home. She greeted the wanderer warmly as though he were an old friend and intimated to him that both she and her husband not only looked forward to his return visit, but truly expected it due to the complexity of the current situation in the kingdom and his inquisitive mind. He left the professor's wife as she busily continued her garden chores and approached the front door of their home. He knocked on the door and within a few short moments the professor appeared. As at their last meeting, the professor greeted him with a hearty handshake, welcomed him into his home, and directed him to the study where he was offered a hot cup of tea. The warmth of his greeting immediately eased any tension he might have had in exploring the various and complex questions that he had organized on his hike. The wanderer began their c onversation by complimenting the professor on his wife's talent and taste in designing the outdoor area of their home. The professor thanked him and directed the wanderer's attention to the subject of the chief of staff and his presentation a few days ear lier. He asked for the wanderer's opinion as to his assessment of the officer's character. Although the wanderer was thrown off course with the direction of their dialogue, the chief of staff's attitude was troubling to him and this was as good a time as ever to discuss it.

"The chief of staff," the wanderer began, "seemed rather dictatorial in his presentation." Although the wanderer agreed that the character of the military was probably dictatorial in nature, it seemed that the chief was not just "suggesting" a strategy to solve the territorial dispute. Rather, "he seemed to be taking charge of the meeting, and frankly," continued the wanderer, "seemed to be not only despotic in his approach, but demagogic and possibly dangerous to the kingdom." The wanderer had chosen his words carefully, understanding that the professor was anticipating and yes, possibly challenging his response. Well, there he said it, he thought to himself, and eagerly awaited the professor's response. As the professor began his reply, the wanderer was aware that not a single word of his evaluation was lost to the professor. The professor took a sip of his hot tea, gave that smile which the wanderer had begun to expect, and indicated that several of his colleagues who were at the meeting agreed with the wanderer's evaluation; however, he continued, the committee was about evenly split on their evaluation of the presentation. Not surprisingly, those who traditionally backed the military were in agreement with the chief of staff's evaluation and strategy regarding the problem. The professor's response was rather ambiguous and the wanderer, struggling to evaluate the professor's position regarding the chief of staff, decided to continue the discussion on a more philosophic level to see if, using this approach, he could evoke a response from the professor that might clarify his position on the matter.

The wanderer began this approach by querying the professor regarding the concept of power and directly related it to the chief of staff. Did he feel, continued the wanderer, that the chief of staff used his position of power in a constructive manner during the meeting the other day, or was his use of power wielded to further aggrandize himself and his personal position?

The professor began his response carefully, and with measured words, perceiving, and rightfully so, that the wanderer was using this line of questioning to deduce his position relative to the chief of staff. "Power", the professor began, "is an intoxicating and complex vehicle that man can use in various ways. Power in its most basic form is man's ability to control other men and situations. In my opinion, one of the basic characteristics of power," continued the professor, "is the desire to be in control of not only oneself, but others with whom one has an association and the situations in which they are involved." The professor indicated that this might be a narrow definition in the eyes of others, but he truly believed it was the correct definition. "As regards the chief of staff and his use of power," the professor, again hedging, indicated that "some people enjoy the use of power more than others, and feel quite comfortable when put in this position, while others hesitate to take on this responsibility and defer to others to whom this is a natural proclivity. How the chief of staff used his position of power was an interpretive judgment, and each individual would have to use his interpretive skills to evaluate the chief of staff. In summary," the professor continued, "the chief of staff obviously enjoyed this position of authority, and his use of this authority required a healthy debate." Again, the professor, using his sharply honed debating skills, avoided positioning himself for or against the chief of staff.

The wanderer digested this measured and calculated response to his question, and decided to continue his dialogue with the professor, addressing the more general issues regarding the state of affairs of the kingdom, which was his reason for this visit. He began, indicating to the professor that during his many visits he had expressed his concern regarding many troublesome conditions of the kingdom. Some of these conditions were of a more serious nature than others, but as a whole they represented a major threat to the survival of the kingdom if they were not addressed in a forthright and deliberate manner. Rather than requesting that the wanderer be more specific regarding which of the problems were of a more serious nature, the professor offered his opinion that there was a direct correlation between the size and complexity of a kingdom and its ability to resolve its problems. The wanderer believed that he understood the professor's interpretation regarding the problems currently facing the kingdom, bu t rather than assume that his interpretation was accurate, he respectfully asked the professor if he would please elaborate on his theory.

The professor began his explanation by asking the wanderer if he did not agree with the basic premise that the larger an entity grew, the more complex it tended to become. This seeming to be a safe assumption, the wanderer agreed with the professor. The professor continued by explaining that the more critical factors in this growth were first, how fast it grew, and second, how the elements participating in the growth interacted. "Concerning the rate of growth," continued the professor, "if the entity grew at a predictable and normal rate, the legislators and other elements of the kingdom could manage the growth. If, however, the growth accelerated beyond this natural growth curve, the results could not only be unpredictable, but potentially disastrous. The variable in this equation was who or what entity could control this rate of growth, and if one were of a cynical mind, was there such an entity?" A thought-provoking question indeed!

The second element of the professor's explanation would not only be as thought-provoking, but at least as challenging. "As the kingdom grew in size, it also grew in complexity. The interaction between these elements is symbiotic, but could become parasitic. As some of the entities grew faster than others, they would become more powerful and influential and would begin to establish an ever-increasing infrastructure. This infrastructure would both build and insulate the entities from outside influence, while at the same time its insatiable quest for growth would lead it to assume a parasitic relationship to other less powerful and influential entities.

On the other side of this unbridled growth would exist those citizens and institutions from which the more 'successful' entities were acquiring wealth and power. They in turn would develop an anti-establishment attitude since they were in the unenviable position of being, figuratively speaking, cannibalized by those who were in power. Again," and the professor stressed this point, "there would always be those who were more successful intellectually, socially, and economically.

This was an unwritten law. When this growth and complexity tumbled out of control, the underclass, which represented the majority in the kingdom, would have no incentive to participate positively in the kingdom's growth. The result would be the inevitable decline of the kingdom over some period of time. If the k ingdom was to survive, it was the duty of that 'invisible hand' within the kingdom to manage a gradual growth and increasing complexity so as to include all citizens. To one degree or another all citizens had to feel that they had a stake in growing the k ingdom with a reasonable chance to fulfill at least a part of their expectations."

Again, the professor had a very perceptive view of the functioning of one of those elements of the kingdom. He obviously enjoyed lecturing regarding his theories of the functioning of the kingdom, and although his dialogue was directed towards the wanderer, the wanderer had the feeling that the professor was on his podium lecturing to his students. As the wanderer absorbed the logical development of the professor's arguments, he could not help but view the intellectual dialogue as representative of the role of the intellectual in the kingdom, namely, to dissect and quantify those aspects of the kingdom, both good and bad, that contributed to its substance. The shortcoming of the intellectual approach to solving those pressing problems of the kingdom was that the intellectual dissected each problem so thoroughly that the answers were in fact not answers, but multifaceted responses, and rather than solve problems, they created more choices. Now this was in fact the rightful role of the intellectual in the kingdom, to identify a problem and construct theoretical solutions, but these theoretical solutions had to be implemented in a practical manner. This would take a different type of mindset, a pragmatic management type. The solution would become even more complex when the political interpretations of these problems were added to the intellectual and pragmatic decisions required. This political element would be the most difficult to quantify since it defied a logical analysis and its solution would be at the crux of any permanent solution to the ills of the kingdom.

The wanderer was now finally beginning to see the complexity of the problems facing the kingdom. By the expression on his face, the wanderer knew that the professor, through the development of his cumulative arguments over their several meetings, had revealed the devilishly complex nature of the current state of affairs.

The professor also perceived in the wanderer's face that the solution to this devilish problem was not in the hands solely of intellectuals like himself, but various citizens with other disciplines. The wanderer and his colleague the professor had finally arrived at a place in their relationship where they had an understanding, and this understanding was not only verbal, but intuitive.

The wanderer thought to himself that to ensure the survival of the kingdom, if in fact this was possible, a solution would have to evolve from not only the intelligentsia, but in conjunction with citizens with other disciplines.

The protective shell of the kingdom was indeed quite thin and vulnerable. Its current structure allowed it to survive the various and complex problems with which it had to cope daily; however, beneath that structure, existed the essence of the kingdom, namely, the individual citizens. Their belief in the structure was critical to its survival and that belief was indeed brittle. Should it become shattered, it was a foregone conclusion that the shell would collapse and anarchy and dissolution of the kingdom would be the result.

As the wanderer left the professor that day, there was a mutuality of respect both by the professor and the wanderer. Each finally understood the impact of their meetings and the perplexing dilemma it had exposed through their discussions. His walk back to the inn that day was both long and thoughtful. With his head hung low and in deep contemplation, he would need time to evaluate all that had passed.

That night after his repast at the inn, he retired to his room where he would spend a night which, although restless as in past nights, produced a serenity in his being. Finally it was revealed to him that knowledge for which he had been searching during his many days an d travels throughout the kingdom. Certainly each of the citizens had a portion of the truth, as he or she perceived it, and a logical solution that would satisfy his or her perception of the problem. However, it was merely a part of the larger dilemma fa cing the kingdom. Certainly some citizens had a better grasp of the larger problems of the kingdom and a correspondingly more comprehensive solution to the possibly more serious problems. Through his dialogue with each citizen, the wanderer was able to deduce the most comprehensive answer to his or her perception of the problems, but there was a far more objective and pervasive truth regarding both the ills and strengths of the kingdom.

That was the "life force" of the kingdom itself, and though inanimate, its perception of the strengths and weaknesses of the kingdom was many times more circumspect, introspective, and objective than any individual or group of citizens in the kingdom. Its truth was constantly evolving and ongoing as individual citizens were born, matured, and died. This cumulative truth was the real essence of the kingdom's "life force." Only from the "life force" could come real and permanent, or evolving as the case may be, resolution to the ills of the kingdom. A successful procedur e to connect with this "life force" would be the critical challenge facing the citizens of the kingdom, and its outcome would certainly determine the kingdom's ultimate survival.

Chapter XV

he wanderer was up at the break of dawn the next morning. There was a spring in his step as he left the inn, a result of the introspective thought process that he had experienced the night before. With his newly enlightened insight into the problems facing the kingdom, he decided to revisit once again those places where he had gathered his experience.

He began his journey at the palace, which was most appropriate. It was at the palace that he experienced his first contact with what would turn out to be only one of the multitude of problems that faced the kingdom. As he approached the gates, he once again crossed the expansive palace grounds and entered the legislative hall. Although he had been there on many occasions in the past, he still could not help but be impressed with the grand design and opulent appearance of the hall and the splendid manner in which its legislators were attired. Although the visiting citizens were obviously not the same citizens he had encountered in the past and the legislators appearing that day were from different constituencies, th e grand theatrical display was the same. He marveled at how these legislators could repeat their compelling performance each day, regardless of the audience present or the agenda that was being addressed. This was both the strength and weakness of the pr ocedure. On the one hand, stability of the kingdom was maintained through this predictable and reliable format. But at the same time, it ensured that any real change to the existing structure was obviated due to the enlightened self-interest of those legislators who were protecting their position in the kingdom. Although some change was occurring through this process, the wanderer was concerned about the trend of the increasing role of the ruling caste, for lack of a better word, and its inevitable flow towards an inequitable, and probably intolerable, balance between the rulers and the ruled in this mostly parasitic relationship.

Upon returning to the inn, he encountered the elderly citizen to whom he had spoken on several occasions. As he approached, h e noticed a calmness, or maybe reluctant acceptance, in his demeanor, which was both comforting and distressing. On the one hand, the elderly citizen had been surviving all of the rapid changes occurring about him without any visible effect on either his lifestyle or his response to these changes. On the other hand, he seemed to be in a stupor and oblivious to the possible ramifications of the rapid changes. Again, if this was the prevailing ethos of the general citizenry, the rulers had lulled the citiz ens into a trance or stupor. The legislative process was being implemented on an unsuspecting citizenry who were being led down a one-way path that might lead to the decline and fall of this kingdom, which ironically would include the rulers. It was not so unique a process, for had this not occurred in other civilizations in the past?

Before he parted company with the elderly citizen, the wanderer queried him as to the condition of his son and his family whom he had met earlier. The elderly citizen sat up in his seat and with a concerned countenance began to divulge what he perceived as growing problems in his son's household. "Each time I visit my son's family it seems," he continued, "they are squabbling more frequently. The two issues that are most outstanding are first, financial concerns, and second, the time, or lack thereof, the parents are able to spend with their children. The harder both husband and wife work and the more money they earn, the more the quality of their family life deteriorates." What an absurd state of affairs, thought the wanderer. What was apparently emerging was that their expectations, mostly economic, were rising at a faster rate than their ability to earn income to support their rising lifestyle. In addition, they had less and less time to spend not only with each other, but with their children. "Now this is not lost on the children", continued the elderly citizen. "They are well aware of the increasing conflict between their parents, for they are contributing to this deterioration of the family. Their only response, given their inability to resolve their parents' problems, is to turn more and more to their peers, whose families, in many cases, are experiencing the same problems." Whether or not this was one of the major problems developing in the kingdom was not as important as the fact that it was one of the accumulating problems, the sum of which was of concern to the wanderer.

As he was discussing the problems of the elderly citizen's son and his family, his thought s began to focus on the problems of children in general, and specifically as related to his previous visit with the superintendent of the school system and the young student whom he interviewed. He recalled the discussion regarding lack of parental supervision and its ramifications, as related to him by the youngster. He decided to visit that place where he could observe, firsthand, the behavior of the children as they interacted in an atmosphere where they would be sharing each other's experiences and articulating those feelings to peers with minimal participation, if any, by adult citizens. That place would be the school.

It was within short walking distance from the inn, and the day was quite pleasant so the wanderer headed in the direction of the scho ol. His walk was made interesting by the presence of several groups of students of various ages heading towards the school with him. As he passed them, they were oblivious to his presence and were in a world of their own. Their discussions were open, an d as he observed in the past their language was both profane and grammatically bizarre. He wondered to himself how this generation of students whom he encountered, if representative of youth in general, could possibly fill those positions in the kingdom to ensure its survival. What was most disturbing to him was that their behavior as a group seemed to flow to the lowest possible denominator. Their dress and language was not even minimally acceptable to standards that would seem appropriate in the adult culture of the kingdom. He wondered to himself, at what point did this behavior by the youth become acceptable to both parents and teachers? At what point was the moral compass lost? Again, finding the answer would be both enigmatic and challenging, and the answer might be much more complex due to the multitude of other changes occurring in the kingdom over such a short period of time.

As he neared the school, he encountered many more students of all ages. His initial impressions were simply reinforced by the almost identical behavior and dress of most all of the students. He did realize that at this age, conformity and imitation of their peers was paramount in the eyes of most of the students. However, his belief in the survival of the kingdom was somewhat reinforced by a small percentage of students who exhibited more normal and acceptable behavior. Maybe this was the circle of students who would play an active role in delivering the kingdom from its current malaise.

On this positive note, he decided to return to the inn, for the hour was growing late, and he had exhausted most of his intellectual energy retracing the footsteps of his journey. He would spend the next day completing the journey and hopefully identify the "life force" of the kingdom.

Chapter XVI

he foreign relations crisis in the kingdom was uppermost on his mind the next morning as he departed the inn after a relatively calm night. The rested wanderer stepped out and directed himself to the local inn outside the palace, the inn he had visited several times before. He had reasonable expectations of finding many of the local legislators having their morning repast. This morning, the inn was alive with activities. Since his last visit to the military affairs committee, the kingdom's military had indeed initiated a "defensive" action into the neighboring kingdom and established its predominance over that area. The discussion, and it was indeed heated, seemed to be how next to proceed. In a sense, this military and political confrontation was at once the most exciting and dangerous combination of citizens, for it in large part determined the direction of the kingdom in any given period. The wanderer's eyes immediately focused on a table in the rear of the inn where his old friend the legislator and the chief of staff were seated. Both of these citizens had major roles in setting the overall policy of the kingdom. He neared the table closely enough to hear their conversation, while at the same time remained inconspicuous so as not to interfere with what appeared to be a heated discussion. The chief of staff was defending the military's position: to consolidate their gains and maintain control over the newly acquired territory. The elderly legislator, on the other hand, was resolutely defending a more balanced position of moving back to the original borders, having succeeded in eliminating the threat and alerting the neighboring kingdom that no further incursions into its territory would be tolerated.

The battle between the military and the more moderate wing of the legislature, as represented by the elderly citizen, displayed both the strength and weakness of the rule in the kingdom. The fact that open debate was encouraged certainly spoke well of this form of rule. But along with this advantage came the darker side of this liberal system, namely, the possible emergence of a demagogue who could use the system and his persuasive powers to dictate current policy. The demagogue could manipulate the system to create a short-term benefit for himself, which might, from a longer perspective, create a dilemma for the kingdom, a conquered territory with its citizens in a state of disruption and the disputed territory festering like a wound. Again, this was another of those challenges facing the kingdom.

As he left the inn, the heated discussions were continuing and the wanderer thought about the human condition, its strengths and frailties, and this remarkable humanly constructed kingdom with its contradictions. Again he pondered the "life force" and its part in this delicate balance.

His fond memories of his visit to the immigrant complex and his meeting with the immigrant family determined that he should make one final visit to the immigrant complex. Since it was a short distance from the inn he had just departed, he directed himself there. Upon approaching the entrance to the immigrant community, the familiar aromas of the exotic delicacies brought warm recollections. He thought that this new influx of immigrants could enrich and broaden the existing culture of the kingdom if the process was implemented gradually and comfortably for both the immigrants and the natural citizens. Hadn't previous immigrations added to the rich essence of the kingdom? The complexity of this process flooded his mind as he mentally revisited his travels throughout the kingdom, noting the many and diverse other issues and the interrelated nature of these problems. His mental attitude was quite positive this day, however, and as he encountered many of the new citizens in the complex, both young and old, he saw that healthy amalgam of both cultures. As he mingled with the new citizens he could scrutinize both the change and resiliency of the newly arrived immigrants. The successful actualization of this process was paramount to building and reinvigorating the kingdom. How this process was managed, not only by the rulers, but by both the immigrants and existing citizens of the kingdom, would determine in large part its successful evolution.

The wanderer was also quite aware that within this equation existed the possibility of the human experiment going awry. The delicate process could be pushed in the wrong direction if the immigrant citizens did not understand how the process of assimilation occurred in the kingdom, something he had noted in his previous visit. However, his outlook today was optimistic, and as he left the complex he felt confident in the goodness of the immigrant citizens in general and of their ability to understand their role in the evol ution of the kingdom and the process of change and its rhythm.

The day was growing short, and the appropriate place to complete his journey would be the church, the moral center of the kingdom. His approach to the church grounds seemed quite prophetic. The cathedral was framed by the setting sun and its framing seemed to portray the church as the center of the kingdom, at least in a spiritual sense. As he neared the cathedral, the stained glass reflected a multicolored appearance that seemed surrealistic, drawing the wanderer in. The professor had revealed to him several days earlier that the elderly minister had since been replaced by a younger minister whose enthusiasm, according to the professor, instilled new life into the religious following. This enthusiasm seemed to be reflected in the physical presence of the religious structure. Perhaps, thought the wanderer to himself, a new awakening was at hand. As he departed the church, the ever-lengthening shadows cast by the edifice directed him back to the inn where he would pass into a deep and uninterrupted slumber.

In his repose that night, he soared high above the kingdom where he could survey it and have full view of the delicate and intricate interrelationship between man and the structures that he had forged, a miraculous fete indeed!

The grand meeting hall had always impressed the professor....But even the richness of this grand hall this morning was overshadowed by the legion of citizens who were gathering....

Chapter XVII

he kingdom was welcomed the following morning by a most magnificent sunrise. Rain had fallen during the night, but by dawn the clouds were clearing. The sun shining through the few remaining scattered clouds gave a warm, pink tone to the countryside, and the cooling breeze blowing across the land gave the air a fresh and sweet aroma. This would be a truly special day.

At his residence, the professor arose and noted on his calendar of events for the day that he was to attend a conference at the grand meeting hall at the church. He did not remember the specifics of the meeting, for he was subject to many such meetings because of his busy schedule. He therefore methodically pursued his morning chores so as not to be late for his appointment.

Since the grand meeting hall at the church was on the grounds of the university, as was the professor's residence, the walk there on this beautiful morning was exhilarating. Upon nearing the grounds of the church, the professor noted that there were many citizens who were also approaching with him, which was quite surprising since this was not a day of worship. He was overwhelmed at the magnitude of those citizens approaching the grand meeting hall. He recognized many of the leading citizens of the kingdom, but there was a significant presence of the general citizenry, including the old, young, and even infirmed. Something extraordinary was about to occur this morning at the grand meeting hall, and as the professor neared the entrance, he became aware of a cacophonous mixture of voices from the citizens gathered inside.

The grand meeting hall had always impressed the professor, for he had been there on many occasions in the past. Its internal arches spiraling upward and its narrow, elongated windows pointing towards the heavens added to the majesty of the structure. The finely finished wooden benches and magnificent portraits that adorned the walls added a richness, which truly made it a grand hall. But even the richness of this grand hall this morning was overshadowed by the legion of citizens who were gathering and the aura of expectancy that permeated the hall.

The professor entered and almost immediately was engulfed by the sea of citizens who continued to pour in. This grand meeting hall had suddenly been reduced not only in size, but also in importance as the massive outpouring of citizens in attendance obscured it. As he mingled with the assemblage of citizens, he could discern parts of their dialogue; however, no one, it seemed, was cognizant of why they were in attendance. A very peculiar circumstance. His eyes were drawn to a group of young citizens who were preoccupied with their particular perspective. As he neared them, his attention focused on one of the young citizens who seemed to have captured the attention of the ot her youths in this group. As was the case with the larger assemblage of citizens, the discussion was centered on the purpose for this massive meeting. The countenance of the young leader, unlike many of those in this group, was more mature and conservati ve in appearance. Rather than expressing the common view of his peers, he proffered a distinctive perspective that gained the attention of not only his peers, but also all of those citizens within range of his presentation. As he continued, he intimated that "although I can not recall the particulars for my attendance this morning, my best recollection is that there is to be a critical town meeting concerning the condition of the kingdom." Having said that, he continued, commenting, "The youth in the kin gdom are in a general state of instability bordering on lawlessness. In past years, the youth had relied on their parents and other elders to give them guidance and leadership. This leadership, due to the current state of affairs and the adult citizens' inability to even cope with their own affairs in an orderly manner, left the youthful, and yes, immature younger citizens to create their own sub-system, which is not only failing miserably, but also deteriorating to the point where it is becoming a major element in the breakdown and decline of the kingdom. If no one else can take control of this developing atrophy, it is the responsibility and duty of the young citizens themselves to take measures to stabilize and reconstruct that portion of the kingdom of which they, by default, are in control." The professor listened in wonderment to the monumental presentation by the youthful leader. How could a youth acquire so much wisdom and leadership quality at such an early age? Perhaps this was one of the sparks that would ignite the radical change required if the kingdom were to survive.

The spontaneous applause as a result of this truly unique presentation was followed by an impromptu and unconstrained eruption of discussions by many of the citizens in attendance. What was most unique about these spontaneous discussions was that they were taking place between groups of citizens who would not ordinarily be discussing problems together. Young and old, rich and poor, and any other combination of citizens were talking to each other and discussing each other's problems and how these problems had a universal basis. A floodgate had been opened and the outpouring of emotions was not only a unique occurrence to the professor, but awakened in him his early radical day s at the university. What was developing before his very eyes was the realization by all groups present that a problem that they thought was unique to their group was, in fact, an intricate combination of problems that were common across all levels of the kingdom. Each problem was an issue not only for those directly affected, but also groups indirectly affected as well. The result was not one problem, but a combination of problems, and the level of complexity was compounded as each group began to discus s the fact that all of their problems were interrelated. A solution could only be arrived at by a united effort that would involve a perspective that they had not envisioned to date, namely, looking at the problem through the eyes of others.

The professor's attention turned to a large gathering of citizens involved in a heated but friendly discussion. As he approached the group, to his amazement there was a robust mixture of both established and newly arrived immigrant citizens. He had, of course, seen many individual encounters between individual immigrants and established citizens, and even small groups of both types of citizens involved in discussions for whatever reason, but he had never seen this magnitude of a mixed gathering of citizens.

His attention was drawn to one of the middle-aged citizens who had obviously been a citizen of the kingdom for many years. At the moment he had the attention of the large gathering, and was discussing his parents, who first arrived in the kingdom many years earlier, and their struggle to gain acceptance as true citizens of the kingdom. He was explaining the indignities they had suffered during their early years as new citizens, and the journey they took to raise a family, educate their children in the new way of life, and the desire for their children to have more than they were able to acquire in their lifetime. This was the legacy for which they struggled. As he continued, he noted that although his parents adopted the ways of the kingdom out of necessity, they retained much of their cultural ties with the past. He, as the first generation to be born into the new kingdom, retained much less of the old culture, although in deference and respect for his parents, he adhered to certain cultural practices for their b enefit. His children were almost entirely unaware and disinterested in the old culture and had become representative of this new culture, with only superficial ties to the old values. What had been evolving was a process of change and integration from an old culture to a new and more successful model, for wasn't this the original impetus for the immigration into the kingdom? As he continued to observe the group, the professor mused that maybe it was a natural proclivity for a group, once attaining full citizenship, to protect its newly acquired position and defend against new "foreigners" opting for participation in "their" culture.

At this point, one of the darker skinned new immigrants took center stage and picked up on the presentation being set forth by the middle-aged citizen. "Not having made your journey," he began, "although we can sympathize with the history of your family, since we are at this very moment pursuing the identical dream, we do not have the perspective or history to use your family as an absolute model for our dreams and aspirations. However, this kingdom is certainly an outstanding model for us to follow. What is required is faith in a model in which we have opted to participate and the patience to persevere the short-term pain in order to share in the rewards that you have reaped from the struggles of your predecessors. A difficult but essential journey." Even his fellow immigrant citizens applauded this introspective analysis by the immigrant spokesman and reinforced the professor's views that evolution rather than revolution was a realistic possibility.

The discussion between the immigrant citizen and his establishment counterpart exhibited to the professor one of the system's strengths. This infusion of energy by the new immigrant citizens helped to reinvigorate a system which, if left unaltered, would probably atrophy because of its inability to change from within. How ironic that the instability of the newly arriving immigrants supplied the energy that enabled the kingdom t o renew itself and thus maintain stability.

The young minister who was discussing this spectacular gathering with his retired counterpart was keenly observing this outpouring of humanity from the rear of the hall. Neither the young minister in his short experience, nor the elderly minister in his very extended experience, had ever witnessed such a spontaneous eruption of humanity. Both noted that what they were observing was nothing short of miraculous. Was it possible that this momentous event could res tore to the kingdom that primacy of faith over materialism and a return to more spiritual values? The elderly minister, his eyes filled with emotion, thought maybe his prayers had been answered and he could witness in his lifetime a return to the values that had been observed in his youthful days. The energy that he had lost over the many years during the decline of religious values was returning in this one momentous event. Once again there was a sparkle in his eyes as many of the citizens passing close to the ministers shook their hands, and many, with tears in their eyes, shared this emotional and most special time in the kingdom.

The professor was continuing his journey of discovery among the multitude of citizens in attendance when he heard the pound ing of a gavel on the table set up on the platform above the floor of the meeting hall. It was the elderly statesman who spent many hours at the inn having his morning repast and discussing political and other problems of the kingdom with his associates. He pleaded with the gathering to give him their attention. As his resonating voice echoed throughout the meeting hall, the discordant voices of the citizens began to diminish, until finally the quiet resembled the silence that occurs when a minister is a bout to preach to the faithful. "I am as dumbfounded as most of you, my fellow citizens seem to be," he began, "at this momentous gathering today. What has brought all of us together is as mysterious to me as I assume it is to you. The condition of the kingdom has been deteriorating for a number of years and somehow we are gathered here today by some mysterious unifying force to save our precious kingdom. Let me begin", he continued, "by confessing a sad truth about most of us in public life. Years ago , public service was considered an honor and a personal commitment to serve the public," stressing the word "serve." "Over the years, this concept has changed radically due in large part to those of us in public service who have become greedy. What we considered a public duty in past years has evolved into a lucrative career, and quite self -serving in many cases. Our service to the public has become second to our self-advancement and personal gain. The citizens have chosen us as their representatives and we in turn have used this trust to further our own careers while giving lip service to the citizens we represent, at least in recent years." As he continued his presentation, his fellow public servants, including not only legislators, but also highly po sitioned judges and administrators, listened in disbelief, while at the same time became resigned to the fact that the time for renewal had arrived, and hopefully not too late to end this system that catered to a privileged ruling class at the expense of the general citizenry. "The system had deteriorated to the point where this privileged class could realize all of its personal material aspirations in the name of public service," he continued, "while promising a better future for the citizens. The citize ns gave us a special position of trust, and we responded by devising, over a period of time, programs to benefit ourselves and our families that were separate from those programs designated for the general citizenry. How cynical we had become. We carefull y orchestrated an asocial theatrical performance in which we on the one hand promised a system for the benefit of the citizens, while at the same time knew these empty promises would never be fulfilled." The legislators and other public servants listened in stunned silence. For them, this was a forced purification that would prove quite costly, yet they were eager to witness the final chapter of this exposition by the elderly statesman. Finally the citizens witnessed true statesmanship devoid of the flowery rhetoric as presented in past years. What was fascinating for the professor as a more than interested bystander was that once this process had begun, the reluctant acknowledgement by his fellow legislators was transformed into a full acceptance of this historical presentation. Perhaps, thought the professor, man had a natural selfish proclivity, and only when forces outside his realm of influence forced the issue of change did it reluctantly occur.

Chapter XVIII

he elderly statesman had just opene d the door to an inevitable restructuring of the kingdom. He was only beginning, however, and now he would address specific important issues, the resolution of which would be not only necessary, but also critical to the salvation of the kingdom.

He began with the health and welfare programs currently in effect in the kingdom. "From this day forward," he proposed, "all citizens would be on the same programs," and he emphasized "same" to reinforce the concept that no longer would those privileged few in the kingdom have their own health, retirement, and welfare programs. "Now we will all, as citizens of the kingdom, be under one inclusive program." There was an excitement in the hall from one end to the other with increasing outbursts of applause and then an outright standing ovation. The elderly legislator pleaded restraint as he continued.

Next on his list was the term of office for public office holders. "From this day forward, elected public servants would by law only be allowed to serve for three years. This restructuring, along with the equalizing of health, retirement, and welfare benefits to all citizens would ensure that new blood would constantly flow into the ruling body of legislators, and these newly elected guardians of the kingdom could truly maintain its integrity, and in three years would be replaced by new guardians. The continuity and maintenance of the kingdom would be the responsibility of a standing bureaucracy that would have no allegiance to one party or the other. With their benefits being the same as the ordinary citizen, it would be in the legislators' best interest to maintain an efficient and honest government. Some of the outgoing elected legislators would obviously claim that continuance of the public programs initiated during their tenure would not continue as productively should they leave office upon the termination of their tenure, but this has always been the rhetoric of legislators in the past as part of selling themselves to the citizenry. In fact, these productive programs, as the legislators so named them, would not only continue under new legislative leadership, but would be improved considerably, due to the infusion of new blood into the legislature, and of course the support of the ongoing bureaucracy which, after all, has been the backbone of the kingdom and has always been instrumental in implementing public programs." An old club would be broken up under the new system, but that old club was quite self-serving and was the reason for the current state of affairs in the kingdom.

The next subject he would broach was the state of affairs of the family. "One of the cornerstones of the kingdom has always been the family unit of mother, father, and children. This institution in recent years has not only been under attack, but its very existence has been challenged by some of the radical groups in the kingdom. As legislators and guardians of the public welfare our hands have not been clean, in fact, we have been a major contributor to the demise of the family unit in the kingdom. Our constant increasing of taxes to support the insatiable appetite for growth in government has led to a critical imbalance between the public and private sectors. In past years, a reasonable tax on individual citizens could adequately support a government necessary to manage the affairs of the kingdom. Because of this unbridled growth of government, more and more taxes have been required to subsidize an ever-increasing bureaucracy, the result of which has necessitated increased revenues. The condition approached the breaking point when individual citizens could no longer afford the ever-increasing tax burden on the family as currently constructed. The result was that the wife, who historically cared for the family at home, now had to jo in her husband in the workplace to support the accelerated tax burden. The consequence has been cataclysmic on two levels. First, the children at home no longer had a parent present to attend to their needs during this critical phase of their development . Second, on the economic level, the women were now competing for the same jobs with the men in the workplace. This resulted in not only more competition for each job, but allowed owners of businesses, now in an advantageous negotiating position, to stru cture wages in their favor. Advocates for this new family configuration justify the arrangement by indicating that the woman is no longer in an inferior position in the family and has now gained that 'independence' that the husband has enjoyed for these many years. This position must be critiqued for several reasons. First, but for those few exceptions, the husband had never viewed his wife as being in an inferior position; her role as homemaker and primary guardian of their children was equal but differ ent from his position as breadwinner and protector of the family. The advocates for a new family construction base their theories on the exception rather than the rule. To sacrifice an invaluable intact family structure, which has maintained stability in the kingdom for as far back as we can recall, for this new 'independence' is at best questioning the historical development of the family unit, and at worst puncturing that delicate family cocoon and reducing the family unit to anarchy. The stress that the husband had historically assumed as breadwinner in the family was now being shared by the wife, which in turn was leading to deleterious effects on the children." The citizens in attendance, while listening attentively to this historical speech, were simultaneously engaged in small intimate discussion groups, indicating that finally many of the feelings they had concerning this new "independence" were finally being challenged, and that the time had arrived to reconfigure the family on a more realistic and traditional basis and to "reinvent" the family unit.

The powerful and the powerless in attendance could be seen discussing this momentous presentation with each other. There would always be both tiers in the kingdom, but at least at this moment they were discussing together the dire straits in which the kingdom found itself and only together could they solve the problem.

The elderly statesman raised his arms in an appeal for silence so he might finish his historical exposition. He began his summary by observing that, "This was only a beginning to a process that must not only be ongoing, but also would create drastic changes in the manner in which the kingdom had been functioning. The meetings in the legislature for quite a few days into the future will be filled with great anticipation and yes, some bitterness, for none of us," he continued, "cedes power and wealth easily, but the inevitable sea change is upon us and radical restructuring of government is not only imminent, but essential if the kingdom is to remain intact." As he ended his presentation, he apologized for its length, but as he left the podium, a thunderous applause indicated that the citizens fully understood the import of this moment, and the professor could not help but reflect that he had been present at a truly historic gathering. The meeting was finally ending, and deep in his thoughts, the professor mechanically strolled from the church meeting grounds towards his home. The brilliant sunset cast a dreamlike aura across the kingdom , which reflected the feelings of its citizens this consequential day. The professor thought of the complexity of this structure that man had created and the almost insurmountable challenges thrust upon him to ensure its continuity. This was a time for soul-searching, and the professor pondered man's limitations in his quest to create a better society. The incongruity in the equation was that the definition of perfecting the society was always changing as each new generation redefined what was a "good" society and included all of those positive values currently in vogue. The society, however, had a life of its own, which was cumulative over the generations. Man's lifetime was relatively short, and his impact could only affect a short span of time in directing the life of the society. At once a contradiction to the professor. He was certainly privileged to be present at this time when this sea change was occurring, and his presence could substantially contribute to this historical period. But how small he felt as part of this miraculous entity called "society" and how inconsequential was his contribution in his own eyes, understanding that whatever this contribution might be, its only effect would be in this phase of the evolution of the kingdom. His writings would certainly be of use as historians looked back at this period of time, but what a humbling experience, thought the professor. His whole life had been spent in the search for solutions to the problems confronting the kingdom, and all of these efforts, documented through his writings and presentations at the university and during his travels, were but a miniscule part of an evolving societal life that was ongoing and in constant flux. It seemed, the professor thought to himself, that since man was flawed as part of being human, his constructs would in turn be flawed. Although his ideals might be admiral and his aim perfection, it was a never-ending search, which during critical times needed major readjustments to ensure its continuity.

Another key element of this fragile equation crossed the professor's mind, and that was the size of the kingdom. This was no small consideration in evaluating its survival and well-being. Its size was critical to its existence. To this time in the evolution of the kingdom, the population had always been increasing. Certainly there was a critical mass of citizens needed to ensure stability in the kingdom, and up to that point, population growth was acceptable. As an integral part of that growth, a certain perc entage of the population was required to manage the affairs of the kingdom and maintain an orderly growth pattern. This was that necessary population of public servants required to ensure a smooth functioning of the kingdom, and also required to protect it from possible outside threats. Remuneration for this necessary government by way of taxes was an acceptable percentage of the wages of the rest of the citizens. However, at a certain point in that growth pattern, two elements critical to the continuity of the kingdom arose. First, not only was the bureaucracy of the kingdom self-perpetuating, but also it had a natural proclivity to grow and expand its influence. This perpetual growth would become unacceptable as the taxes on citizens to support this ever-growing bureaucracy would reach their capacity to support this behemoth. Second, at a certain point, the population, which was also ever expanding, would have to level off and stabilize, for if this did not occur, all of those dire consequences of overpopulation would eventuate. These were truly monumental potential problems with which previous generations did not have to contend.

His wife, who was as usual, busy in the garden, greeted him with a warm embrace....they would discuss long into the evening the prodigious changes that would be taking place in the kingdom....

Chapter XIX

s he approached his home, he could not help but reflect on how fortunate he was to have his beautiful life partner, his very comfortable home, and his very satisfying care er at the university. His wife, who was as usual, busy in the garden, greeted him with a warm embrace, and told him that along with their evening repast they would be enjoying a fresh garden salad, the ingredients of which she had just hand - picked. Little did she know that this evening as they ate, she would be subject to one of the many eclectic discussions that they shared at their evening meals; however, tonight's discussion would be very special. Not only would he disclose to her the extraordinary events of the day at the church meeting grounds, but they would discuss long into the evening the prodigious changes that would be taking place in the kingdom over the many days into the future, and even how their future would be drastically changed, as woul d that of all other citizens in the kingdom. Both the powerful and the powerless would feel the effect of this tidal change that was about to occur in the kingdom. This change, which would be upon them as early as tomorrow, would reverberate throughout the kingdom, shaking loose all of those traditions established over the years. But as reflected upon earlier, what was a tidal change in the eyes of today's citizens was but a minuscule activity in the ongoing and much larger societal evolution of the kingdom.

Looking down upon the kingdom, as the citizens slept, there was serenity, yet an anticipatory aura over the kingdom, and tomorrow would indeed bring regeneration and a new day.

www.ingramcontent.com/pod-product-compliance
Ingram Content Group UK Ltd.
Pitfield, Milton Keynes, MK11 3LW, UK
UKHW051130260726
13967UKWH00010B/2955